Presented to
Tulsa City-County Library
by the
**Anne V. Zarrow
Library Books
for Children Fund**

Tulsa Community Foundation

tulsa
LIBRARY TRUST

JAN - - 2021

D1613590

The Frog at the Window

by

Scott J. Langteau

illustrated by

Michaela Brannon

Published by Shake the Moon Books
www.shakethemoonbooks.com

ISBN: 978-0-578-55965-0
Copyright 2020 by Scott J. Langteau

Printed in China.

This book is printed in compliance with the
Consumer Products Safety Improvement Act (CPSIA).

All rights reserved. No part of this book may be reproduced in any form
or by any electronic means without permission in writing from the copyright holder.
Reviewers may quote brief passages for review purposes.
This is a work of fiction. All characters and events herein are fictional.

Special Thanks to:
Elizabeth M. Timmins, Jeff Thomas, Michelle Gray
and Vi Truong - without whom this book would not be possible.

Dedicated to our Families,
who always made Christmas magical.

Scott and Michaela

Tonight was the very first storm of the year,
and surprising how much it had snowed.
The Randalls were packed and all ready for bed,
with plans to wake early and then hit the road.

"Now Christmas was only a few days away,"
thought Katy, relaxed by the tree.
"How will we ever reach Grandmother's house,
when it's snowing so hard I can't see?"

And then
as she sat staring into the night,
through the blustery, snowy white fog -
there stood in the cold window's lower right edge,
a tiny, green, shivering FROG.

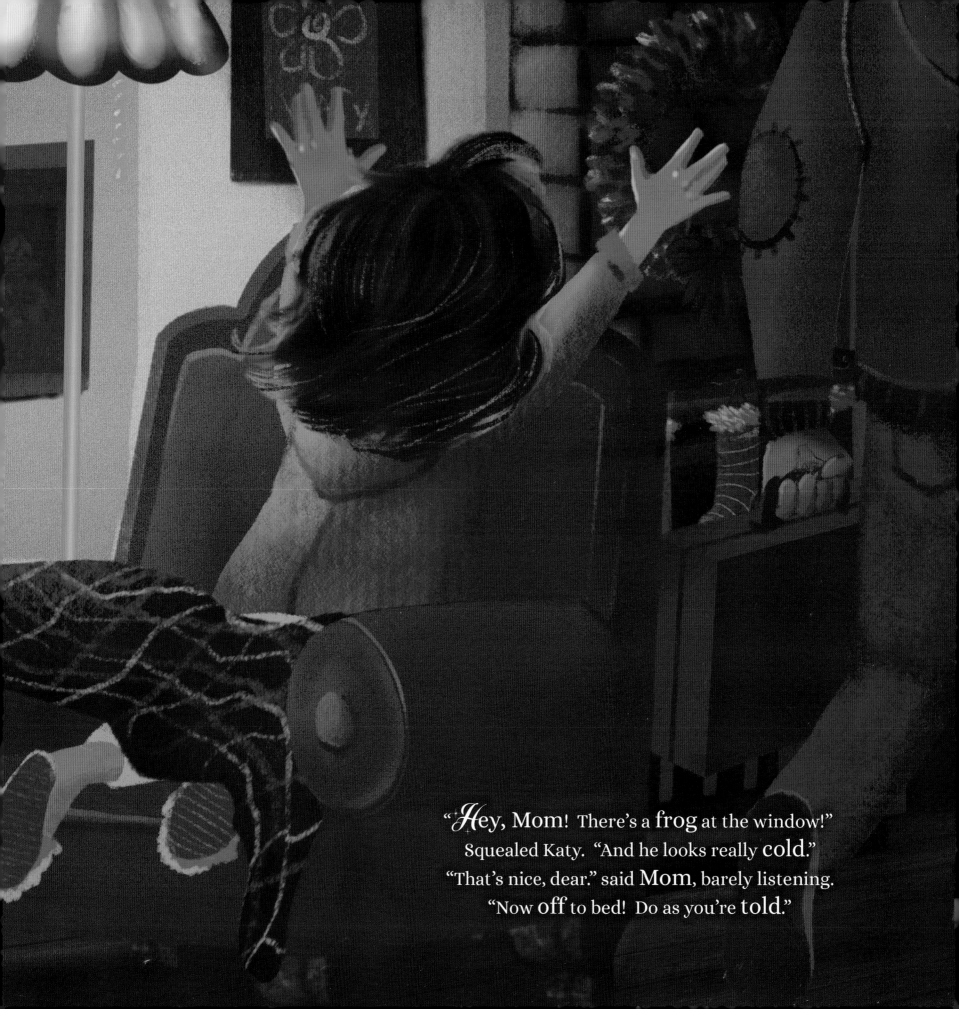

"Hey, Mom! There's a frog at the window!"
Squealed Katy. "And he looks really cold."
"That's nice, dear." said Mom, barely listening.
"Now off to bed! Do as you're told."

At dawn Katy rushed back to the window,

but her green, little friend was no more.

And as Dad took her hand saying: "Come now, we're late!",

her best mitten fell square in the door.

*T*hen as soon as their car **disappeared** on the hill
of their long, yearly vacation **ride**,
the **door** to their warm, empty house left behind...

...opened up
and her FROG
peeked inside!

"Hey now! What have we here?" he croaked to himself.
"It's much nicer than my muddy stream.
There's curtains and carpet and plenty of space!
Bye-bye cold forest, this place is a dream!"

So he **quickly** hopped home and **packed** up his things,
and he **moved them all** into the house.
Then **claimed** the big armchair as **his** favorite spot,
where he **settled in** snug as a mouse.

And speaking of mice, two now stood at the door -
before barging right in with the breeze.

They **jumped** in the armchair and **grabbed** the remote,
changing the show to a special on **cheese!**

Our kind little frog was **surprised**, to be sure,
and was **eager** to tell them to go.
But **their right** to be there was **equal** to his,
so he **sulked** as they **talked** through the show!

When at once Mrs. Mouse sat up with a jolt!
"Is that water? I hear a Blub-Blub!"

They followed the sound to the bathroom nearby...

...where a beaver had built
his dam in the tub!
It was sturdy and proud with a grand waterfall.
"Hey there, new neighbors!" said a beaver's wide grin.
"The location is great and the water is fine!
And the window was open so I let myself in."

Turning and grumbling with a **sense of dismay**,
Froggie saw **footprints** he'd not seen before.
Which **led** to a room at the **end of the hall**,
where he took a **deep breath**...

...and **threw open** the door!

*W*here **settling in** was a family of **bears,**
who were testing the bed **one** at a **time.**
"It's too soft for our backs!" Mom and Dad both agreed.
"WELL THEN!" said Baby, "This ONE is ALL MINE!"

"Hello, little Frog!" growled the big father bear.
"Our bed search has us in a bind.
We sleep through the winter - as you likely know,
and this man-cave is ONE SWEET, SWEET find!"

Froggie sighed
and trudged back to his armchair,
no longer sure what he might face.

Where to his wide eyes,
some rabbits were running.
That's right!
They were deep in a race!

A stern owl perched its nest in the bookshelf.
Two fat squirrels had laid claim to the tree.
A snoring red fox lay asleep in the dog bed –
plainly drooling for the whole house to see!

It's then our frog **knew**
    they **were all** there to stay,
as they **rushed** about acting like **fools**.

So to **save** his new home,
    he gathered them up
and **together** laid down some **house rules**.

Rule 1: Simply put - do your business outside!

Rule 2: Keep your room neat and clean.

Rule 3: One they couldn't stress strongly enough...

...trying to eat someone else is just mean!

Rule 4: No loud music beyond 10 P.M.

Rule 5: Fix what you break, my dear!

Rule 6: And perhaps most important of all...

JAN 1

Back from Grandma's House!

...everyone out by the first of the year!

*T*hen they **all** set their thoughts
on the **big holiday**
and each **helped** deck the halls
in their style.

Before **planning a party**
(the best of the year)...

...that would beat Halloween by a MILE!

And soon, just like that -
Christmas Day had arrived
and their lives felt like one giant treat.

They sang and they danced,
and exchanged simple gifts.

But what they did mostly was EAT!

'Then all of a sudden the fun came to a halt
as some humans strolled up to the yard!
Where one stood and stared at the house for a while
as the other scrawled notes on a card.

"We have to do something! They've seen us for sure!"
Whispered Frog voicing all that they feared.
So they all struck a pose in a "Christmasy" scene...

...for which the only description is weird!

*B*ut it worked!
They **left**, and the **party** raged on...

(Once they quickly closed
every last shade.)

Then **at last** they grew tired and each **crawled** into bed –
so in **love** with the **home** they had made.

Now it's true, you know, that old phrase that they say?
That all GOOD things must come to an END.

18
24
25
GRANDMA'S
HOME AGAIN!!
31
Grandma's

Soon the date on the wall
said it's near time to go –
so pack up and hug every new friend.

They cleaned and they scrubbed and re-ordered the house.

Yes, even the dam pulled its plug!

They **woke up** the bears and **re-laundered** the sheets –

and they **hid** the **big stain** in the rug!

And just as the Randalls' car rolled up the drive,
as though it were destined by fate,
every critter and creature had now up and gone –
leaving Froggie to close the rear gate.

"Hey, Mom! I found it
  – my lost mitten's right here!"
Squealed Katy
    as she reached the top stair.

"Well, aren't you lucky?"
    said Mom with a smile.
"It was Gram-Gram
    who knit you that pair!"

Oh so glad to be home, the Randalls relaxed,
but the house simply didn't feel right.
The couch cushions sagged, there was fur on the towels –
and the water bill gave Dad a fright!

CONGRATULATIONS!
Best Christmas Display!
Most CREATIVE in Town!
Your use of stuffed animals-
WHAT FUN!

But the **oddest** of all things **hung** on the door.
A **Blue Ribbon** announcing they'd **won:**

"BEST CHRISTMAS DISPLAY!

MOST CREATIVE IN TOWN!"

"Your **use** of stuffed animals – WHAT FUN!"

It's then Katy **raced** to a **window** again
and saw **Frog** leave the **scene of the crime**.
She **leaned out** and **yelled** as he hopped toward the woods:

"WELL, I SURE HOPE YOU HAD A GOOD TIME!"

So now every year
when the Holidays call
and the Randalls are packed and away,

Katy makes sure
she has left out her "key"...

…so her friends
have a nice place to stay!

The End.

Yes!
Froggie
really exists!

The original "Frog at the Window" photo that
inspired it all - taken on a cold and rainy night
by librarian extraordinaire Elizabeth M. Timmins
at her home in Wisconsin.

Scott J. Langteau

Growing up in the small town of Seymour, Wisconsin, playtime came ready-made with Scott's 11 brothers and sisters. No lie! Having fun then meant grabbing a sibling, heading outside and imagining a world around you.

That imagination brought Scott Theater degrees from the University of Wisconsin - Stevens Point and Villanova University before bringing him to L.A. where he's worked as a producer, writer and actor for over 20 years. Best known for his work on the highly acclaimed commercial blockbusters "Medal of Honor" & "Call of Duty" game franchises, Scott has done work for companies including Disney, Pixar, DreamWorks, EA Games, and the Jim Henson Company to name a few. He has written three other award-winning children's books: "Sofa Boy", "The Question", and "BULLIED".

The Christmas holiday was always a magical time in the Langteau household. and it has always been a dream of Scott's to bring a Christmas story to life. "The Frog at the Window" has given Scott that opportunity - and he will always be grateful for the curious, little, green intruder and the photo that inspired his story.

Michaela Brannon

Born and raised in Pasadena, California, Michaela Brannon has always had a strong affinity for the creative arts. After attending the California State Summer School for the Arts (C.S.S.S.A.) in 2012 for sculpture and painting, she decided to pursue a career in the field of animation.

She graduated in the spring of 2018 from the Art Center College of Design in Pasadena, California with honors, now holding a BFA in Illustration Entertainment Arts.

When she is not working, Michaela can be found dog whispering, binge watching "Twin Peaks", or spending time with her friends and family.

Also available from Shake the Moon Books
and author Scott J. Langteau

Sofa Boy (Ages 4~8)

A young boy discovers that lounging on his favorite sofa playing videogames around the clock is not all it's cracked up to be. His lack of attention to life's basics such as bathing, good food, fresh air, sunlight, and old fashioned exercise wreaks havoc on his young body, and before long our little lad finds himself a prisoner of his own designing, as well as the fascination of many an onlooker as he becomes literally joined at the hip with his increasingly disgusting environment. Sofa Boy is a funny and beautifully illustrated lesson-learned about moderation ~ a lesson that clearly speaks to all ages, and goes down easily with a warm and hearty chuckle.

The Question (Ages 4~8)

After watching the snowstorm of the season blow into his neighborhood, a young boy wakes to find his town literally buried beneath a mountain of snow. Possibly stuck inside his house for the rest of the winter, survival questions of every shape and size race through his mind ~ including one that tugs at his thoughts to the very end of his adventure. The Question is a wild journey through the mind of a child, with an ending so honestly relatable, you can't help but smile.

BULLIED

A modern day look at middle school bullying. (Ages 9~12)

A modern-day inspired anti-bullying picture book that casts light on a route to self-acceptance and empowerment. Bullied follows the day-to-day struggles of 7 young targets of aggression along with their tormentors from adolescence to adulthood. Through the journey of this book the reader discovers that accepting and staying true to oneself and examining one's behavior and its motivations serve as powerful and empowering messages for both the bullied, and bully alike.